D1005844

NANCY DREW

DREW
girl detective®

TOOLS

SHEYS

PAPERCUTZ™

NANCY
DREW
girl detective
®

#13

Doggone Town

STEFAN PETRUCHA & SARAH KINNEY • Writers
SHO MURASE • Artist
with 3D CG elements and color by CARLOS JOSE GUZMAN
Based on the series by
CAROLYN KEENE

PAPERCUTZ™
New York

Doggone Town
STEFAN PETRUCHA & SARAH KINNEY – Writers
SHO MURASE – Artist
with 3D CG elements and color by CARLOS JOSE GUZMAN
BRYAN SENKA – Letterer
JOHN McCARTHY – Production
JIM SALICRUP
Editor-in-Chief

ISBN 10: 1-59707-098-X paperback edition
ISBN 13: 978-1-59707-098-0 paperback edition
ISBN 10: 1-59707-099-8 hardcover edition
ISBN 13: 978-1-59707-099-7 hardcover edition

Printed in China.
Distributed by Macmillan.

10   9   8   7   6   5   4   3   2   1

GIRL DETECTIVE **NANCY DREW** HERE.

NOTHING LIKE STARTING A MYSTERY WITH A SPOOKY HOUSE IN A THUNDERSTORM, EH? ONLY IN THIS CASE, THE SPOOKY HOUSE IS **MINE.**

OH, IT WOULDN'T BE **NEARLY** AS SPOOKY IF THE STORM HADN'T BLOWN THE LIGHTS OUT, AND MY LAWYER DAD, CARSON DREW, WEREN'T OUT OF TOWN ON BUSINESS!

AND YEAH, THERE IS THAT **SHADOWY FIGURE** POKING ABOUT IN MY ROOM!

LET'S SEE WHO IT IS, SHALL WE?

CHAPTER ONE:
INTRUDER IN THE MUD

HA! FOOLED YOU. IT'S JUST *HANNAH*, OUR HOUSEKEEPER!

NANCY? YOU IN HERE?

SHE'S BEEN SORT OF A MOTHER TO ME AS LONG AS I CAN REMEMBER. ALWAYS WORRIED ABOUT ONE THING OR ANOTHER.

-TRK-

EH?

OF COURSE, IN *THIS* CASE YOU CAN'T BLAME HER FOR BEING A LITTLE ANTSY, WHAT WITH THE STORM, AND THE LIGHTS...

BUT HANNAH'S NOT THE SORT TO BACK DOWN, EVEN WHEN AFRAID, ESPECIALLY IF SHE'S *WORRIED* ABOUT ME.

I'VE ALWAYS *ADMIRED* THAT ABOUT HER...

...EVEN IF, AS THEY SAY, DISCRETION IS SOMETIMES THE BETTER PART OF VALOR.

WHICH MEANS, BASICALLY, SOMETIMES YOU SHOULD *LOOK* VERY CAREFULLY BEFORE YOU *LEAP*.

I'D HAVE **TOLD** HER I WAS FINE IF I'D HEARD HER, BUT I WAS DOWN IN THE BASEMENT DIGGING UP EXTRA FLASHLIGHTS WITH MY PALS **BESS MARVIN** AND **GEORGE FAYNE**.

BESS AND GEORGE ARE SO *DIFFERENT*, I OFTEN HAVE TO REMIND MYSELF THAT THEY'RE *COUSINS*.

SHE SEEMED PRETTY WORRIED.

YOU THINK?

WELL, BETTER GO SEE WHAT SCARED HER.

IS THERE *ANY* POINT IN TELLING NANCY THAT IF HANNAH WAS SCARED, IT COULD BE *DANGEROUS* UP THERE?

NOPE. GIRL DETECTIVE PLUS MYSTERY EQUALS *TROUBLE*.

WHAT'S THAT LIGHT? A UFO?

GEORGE IS RIGHT. I AM ALWAYS GETTING MYSELF INTO TROUBLE. BUT HOW ELSE CAN YOU SOLVE A MYSTERY IF YOU'RE NOT WILLING TO TAKE SOME RISKS?

NO. LIGHTNING. THERE'S A *STORM*, REMEMBER?

AND MY PALS, BLESS 'EM, ARE ALWAYS BEHIND ME. SOMETIMES A FEW *FEET* BEHIND ME, BUT BEHIND ME.

IT'S OKAY, GUYS. I THINK WHATEVER IT WAS IS *GONE*.

HM... BUT MAYBE NOT *TOO* FAR GONE.

THE MUD ON THE FLOOR WAS *DRYING*, BUT THE MUD ON MY BUREAU AND THE SILL WAS STILL *WET*, WHICH MEANT IT WAS *VERY* RECENT.

HANNAH'S "DEVIL" COULD BE RIGHT OUTSIDE IN THE TREE.

WHICH MEANT, OF COURSE, I *HAD* TO FOLLOW.

IT'S NOT AS *DANGEROUS* AS IT LOOKS. NOT FOR ME, ANYWAY. DAD SAYS I WAS CLIMBING THIS TREE SINCE BEFORE I COULD WALK.

OF COURSE, IT PROBABLY WASN'T *RAINING* THEN.

JUST FOR *ONCE* COULDN'T WE HANG OUT AND WATCH A DVD LIKE *NORMAL* PEOPLE?

ELEC-TRICITY'S OUT, REMEMBER?

RIGHT. HOW ABOUT SHADOW-PUPPETS?

WHATEVER IT WAS, UP IN A TALL TREE, WHEN IT LATCHED ONTO MY FACE, WAS DEFINITELY NOT THE BEST PLACE TO BE.

≳GLERP≲

IT WAS EXACTLY TWENTY-THREE FEET, SEVEN INCHES TO THE GROUND. I KNOW BECAUSE I'D MEASURED.

I PROBABLY WOULDN'T *DIE* FROM THE FALL, UNLESS I LANDED FUNNY, BUT A FEW BROKEN BONES WAS A GOOD BET!

≳AHHHH≲

THEN THERE WAS THE QUESTION OF WHAT THE *THING-ON-MY-FACE* HAD PLANNED FOR ME...

HOW'D HE GET IN? DOGS CAN'T CLIMB TREES.

THEY CAN. SORT OF. IF YOU SEARCH FOR "DOG CLIMBING TREE" YOU'LL GET ALL SORTS OF VIDEOS AND PICTURES.

ONCE WE FOUND HANNAH AND TOLD HER WHAT WAS GOING ON, SHE WAS HER OLD SELF AGAIN, INSISTING OUR VISITOR HAVE A BATH IF HE WAS GOING TO STAY IN THE HOUSE!

MOSTLY THEY SORT OF SCRABBLE UP THE MAIN TRUNK, THEN IF THERE'S A THICK FLAT BRANCH, LIKE WITH MY TREE, THEY CAN KEEP GOING.

AND IF THIS LITTLE GUY CAN DO ONE THING, IT'S *SCRABBLE*! YUCK!

AT LEAST HE'S *CLEAN* NOW.

AND LEAN. LOOKS LIKE HE HASN'T EATEN IN A WHILE. IF HE'S A *RUNAWAY* HE'S COME FROM PRETTY FAR.

MAYBE THEY WERE AFRAID TOGO WOULD COME BACK SO THEY *MOVED*.

VERY FUNNY.

MISSING DOG

WHILE NED DID THE OBVIOUS, I WENT IN FOR A CLOSER LOOK.

WINDOW AFTER WINDOW, IT WAS THE SAME. IN ONE HOUSE, THERE WAS STILL FOOD ON THE PLATES.

HELLO! ANYONE?

AS IF EVERYONE HAD LEFT IN A *HURRY*.

SOON THE ONLY HOUSE LEFT WAS THE ONE WE CAME TO FIND IN THE FIRST PLACE.

THIS IS THE STREET! WHERE'S THE OWNER'S HOUSE?

UH....

Lonesome Drive

3rd

I GUESS *THAT'S* IT.

WE BROUGHT THE CAR UP AS CLOSE AS WE COULD.

EVEN THOUGH TOGO WAS ITCHING TO GET OUT, I WANTED TO KEEP HIM IN THE CAR UNTIL I FIGURED OUT WHAT WAS GOING ON. IF HE RAN AWAY ONCE, HE COULD DO IT AGAIN.

THIS PLACE LOOKS EVEN MORE DESERTED THAN THE REST OF THE TOWN.

WELL, LET'S JUST MAKE SURE.

IF NO ONE'S *HOME*, AN OLD SHACK LIKE THIS SHOULD BE *EASY* TO GET INTO.

MAYBE I CAN FIND SOME...

...CLUES?

YEAH?

B-BYRA TUSSLE?

SHE HAD A TIRED, WORN FACE, FULL OF WORRIES, WHICH I GUESS I COULD UNDERSTAND IF THIS LITTLE SHACK WAS HER HOME.

YEAH.

HER DRESS WAS LITTLE MORE THAN GRAY RAGS.

WHICH MADE IT EVEN *STRANGER* FOR HER TO BE WEARING SUCH AN *EXPENSIVE* WRISTWATCH!

WELL?

I DON'T HAVE ALL DAY...

WHAT DO YOU WANT?

WE... WE'RE FROM RIVER HEIGHTS WE FOUND YOUR DOG, TOGO! HE'S IN THE CAR!

YOU FOUND IT?

THAT'S IMPOSSIBLE!

I'M NOT USED TO HAVING A DOG AROUND, SO I FORGOT ONE OF THE BASIC RULES.

NEVER LEAVE YOUR PET ALONE IN A CAR.

THERE ARE *LOTS* OF REASONS FOR THIS RULE.

ESPECIALLY IF YOU DRIVE A MANUAL TRANSMISSION.

FOR ONE THING, THE PET MIGHT ACCIDENTALLY HIT THE *STICK SHIFT* AND PUT THE CAR IN *NEUTRAL*.

WE'D JUST ABOUT MANAGED TO CONVINCE BYRA THAT WE WEREN'T DOG-NAPPERS, WHEN I HEARD A STRANGE *SOUND*.

LIKE TIRES ON A *GRAVEL* ROAD.

AND I REALIZED THAT EVEN THOUGH I'D REMEMBERED THE GAS, I'D *FORGOTTEN* TO PUT ON THE EMERGENCY BRAKE!

END CHAPTER ONE

FORTUNATELY, THE CAR WASN'T MOVING *TOO* FAST YET. NED AND I WOULD *PROBABLY* BE ABLE TO CATCH UP WITH IT.

BUT WHEN MY FREE-ROLLING HYBRID SLIPPED INTO SOME OVERGROWTH?

SOMEONE GOT UPSET.

NO!

DON'T TOUCH IT!

FROM THE WAY BYRA **SCREAMED**, I FIGURED THERE WAS A PIT OF **RATTLESNAKES** ON THE OTHER SIDE OF THAT BRUSH!

SO WE JUST **FROZE**.

AND EVEN THOUGH BYRA LOOKED TIRED AND OUT OF SHAPE...

...SHE COULD REALLY **MOVE** WHEN SHE WANTED TO!

WE REALLY SHOULD HAVE RUSHED TO HELP, BUT WE WERE BOTH PRETTY SURPRISED BY BYRA'S FEROCITY.

SHE WAS LIKE A TIGER CHARGING A GAZELLE.

AND YOU REALLY DIDN'T WANT TO GET IN HER WAY WHEN SHE POUNCED.

NOW, I DRIVE A *HYBRID CAR*, WHICH IS VERY EFFICIENT. ASIDE FROM THE BATTERY-ASSISTED ENGINE, IT SAVES ON GAS BECAUSE IT'S SO *LIGHT*.

SO YOU REALLY DON'T HAVE TO BE *SPIDER-MAN* OR ANYONE LIKE THAT TO STOP IT FROM ROLLING DOWN A SMALL HILL.

EVEN SO, BYRA WAS PRETTY *IMPRESSIVE*.

BY THE TIME SHE ACTUALLY STOPPED THE CAR, NED AND I WERE COMING OUT OF SHOCK.

DO YOU...

...WANT SOME *HELP*?

NO! STAY BACK!

I WAS SO DISTRACTED, I WAS AFRAID I'D FORGET TO *BREATHE.*

I HAD A FEELING THAT THIS TIME, NED, WHO'S USUALLY PRETTY MUC FOCUSED, FELT THE SAME WAY.

AT LEAST TOGO AND THE CAR LOOKED NO WORSE FOR WEAR.

≥*URPHH!*≤

SO, ANYWAY...

THE REASON WE DROVE ALL THIS WAY IS BECAUSE *THIS* FRISKY FELLOW WOUND UP IN MY BEDROOM!

HIS DOG-TAG GAVE YOUR ADDRESS. BUT I WAS A LITTLE SURPRISED THERE WAS NO PHONE LISTED!

THAT WAS A SUBTLE INVITATION FOR BYRA TO EXPLAIN WHY THERE WAS NO PHONE LISTING.

HOW'S MY DOG? EH? HOW YOU BEEN?

GRRRRRRRRRR!

OW!

WHY YOU MANGY...

SNAP

THAT WAS THE SECOND FACE I'D SEEN THIS TREE-CLIMBING DOG LEAP ON.

I CAN'T IMAGINE WHY ANYONE WOULD *TRAIN* A DOG TO DO SOMETHING LIKE THAT.

BUT DOGS ARE PRETTY SMART. MAYBE LITTLE TOGO JUST FIGURED OUT IT WAS AN EASY WAY TO DEAL WITH *PESKY* HUMANS.

IN ANY CASE, ASIDE FROM EVERY-THING ELSE STRANGE ABOUT HER, I WAS NOW *CONVINCED* BYRA WASN'T TOGO'S OWNER.

*'ℰˆ#✇$!# MONGREL!

I ALSO DIDN'T CARE FOR HER UNNECESSARY, THOUGH COLORFUL, *LANGUAGE*.

STILL, I DIDN'T HAVE ANY *PROOF*.

DID HE BREAK THE SKIN? ARE YOU HURT?

GET AWAY FROM ME! I'M *FINE*!

UNLESS YOU CONSIDER A REALLY *JUICY* MYSTERY A REWARD!

WE'RE NOT GOING TO STAY AWAY FOR OUR OWN GOOD, *ARE* WE?

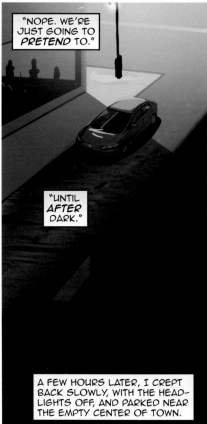

"NOPE. WE'RE JUST GOING TO *PRETEND* TO."

"UNTIL *AFTER* DARK."

A FEW HOURS LATER, I CREPT BACK SLOWLY, WITH THE HEAD-LIGHTS OFF, AND PARKED NEAR THE EMPTY CENTER OF TOWN.

AND WHAT SELF-RESPECTING DETECTIVE WOULDN'T HAVE A FLASHLIGHT HANDY?

I ALSO HAD A *SPARE* FOR NED, BUT, REALLY, YOU'D THINK HE'D KNOW ENOUGH TO BRING HIS *OWN* BY NOW.

BUT EVEN *MY* FIRST GUESSES AREN'T ALWAYS RIGHT.

AND SOON I HAD ANOTHER DISTRACTION.

RUFF!

TOGO!

WHERE IS HE? WHERE'D HE GO?

QUIET DOWN! WE SHOULD BE ABLE TO HEAR HIS LITTLE FEET ON THE GRAVEL.

AND SURE ENOUGH, THERE HE WAS!

IF I DIDN'T KNOW BETTER, I'D SWEAR HE WAS TRYING TO LEAD US SOMEWHERE!

AND, IN POINT OF FACT, I *DIDN'T* KNOW BETTER!

AT FIRST I WAS AFRAID HE'D HEAD FOR BYRA'S SHACK, BUT INSTEAD, TOGO MADE A *BEE-LINE* (OR MAYBE A DOG-LINE?) FOR THE FAR-SIDE OF THE CEMETERY.

NED, KEEP THE FLASHLIGHT BEAM *LOW!* WE DON'T WANT BYRA TO SEE US OUT HERE!

HE'S NOT GOING TO TRY TO DIG UP ANY BONES, IS HE?

LET'S HOPE NOT.

THE LITTLE GUY DOES SEEM TO HAVE SOMETHING *SPECIFIC* ON HIS MIND.

LIKE THIS PARTICULAR *GRAVE-STONE!*

YOU COULD SLOW *DOWN* A LITTLE, Y'KNOW!

SHHHH!

FOR A SECOND, IT LOOKED LIKE SOMETHING WAS FLASHING A LIGHT *BACK* AT US!

YEESH! WHAT'S *IN* THERE!

WAIT! WHERE ARE YOU *GOING?*

IT'S OKAY.

I THOUGHT MAYBE THE TOWNFOLK WERE *IN* HERE, HAVING THEIR *PARTY*.

I WAS THINKING THE SAME THING, ONLY THERE WAS SOMETHING ABOUT THE CAVE THAT WAS ALMOST TOO *GOOD* TO BE TRUE!

AND THEN I NOTICED TOGO DIGGING AT THE BASE OF ONE OF THE BIGGER, MORE COLORFUL CAVE FEATURES.

STALAGMITES RISE *UP* FROM A CAVE FLOOR, FORMED BY DRIPPING WATER, FILLED WITH MINERALS, FROM THE CEILING.

STALACTITES, ARE FORMED THE SAME WAY, ONLY THEY GROW *DOWN* FROM THE CAVE CEILING.

WHATEVER TOGO WAS DIGGING AT WENT FROM THE FLOOR ALL THE WAY UP TO THE CEILING, KIND OF LIKE A *SUPPORT BEAM*.

NOW, STALACTITES AND STALAGMITES OFTEN MEET AND FORM ONE "ITE" THING, BUT THAT TAKES HUNDREDS OF THOUSANDS OF YEARS.

IT'S **ALL** PLASTIC!

THIS CAVE ISN'T **NATURAL**! IT'S ALL A **FAKE**!

WHICH WASN'T TO SAY THAT THE PARTICULAR FAKE FORMATION TOGO WAS DIGGING AT WAS TOTALLY USELESS.

MATTER OF FACT, IT **WAS** A **SUPPORT** BEAM!

AND THE **CAVE-IN** THAT STARTED WHEN IT FELL? THAT WAS **COMPLETELY** REAL!!

END CHAPTER TWO

A MISSING TOWN, A FAKE CAVE, AND A GHOST? THIS IS CRAZY, NANCY! IT'S NOT EVEN LIKE PIECES OF THE SAME MYSTERY.

ACTUALLY, IT'S STARTING TO MAKE *TOTAL* SENSE!

BEFORE POOR NED COULD QUESTION MY SANITY, I WAS UP AND RUNNING, BACK TOWARD *BYRA'S*.

AND OF COURSE, CRAZY OR NOT, NED JUST *FOLLOWED*.

HE'S REALLY A *GREAT* GUY, ISN'T HE?

LOOK! THERE'S A SMALL *GAP* IN THE COLLAPSED STONES! TOGO'S HEADING IN! IT LOOKS JUST BIG ENOUGH FOR ME, TOO!

NANCY, DON'T EVEN *THINK* ABOUT IT...

OKAY, I WON'T THINK! I'LL JUST *DO* IT!

NO! NANCY, THOSE ROCKS ARE STILL *LOOSE!*

UNFORTUNATELY, NED WAS *RIGHT!*

NANCY!

CRUNK!

MOVING VERY CAREFULLY, I MADE MY WAY THROUGH WHAT I WAS SURE WAS A *REAL* CRYSTAL CAVE.

I COULD TELL IT WAS REAL BECAUSE THE CRYSTAL NOT ONLY *GLOWED*, IT TORE MY SHIRT AS I RUBBED PAST IT.

RRIIIIPP

SO FAR, THE SECOND CAVE CONFIRMED *ONE* OF MY SUSPICIONS.

AND WHAT I SAW *NEXT* CONFIRMED ANOTHER!

SORRY. NOT EXACTLY. THE ENTRANCE *COLLAPSED* WHEN I CAME IN!

BUT MY BOYFRIEND NED'S GETTING HELP, SO WE SHOULD ALL BE RESCUED VERY SOON!

THANK *HEAVENS!* WE'VE BEEN HERE FOR *DAYS!*

OUR FLASHLIGHT BATTERIES BURNED OUT YESTERDAY!

YOU FOUND *TOGO!*

YEP, ALL THE WAY IN RIVER HEIGHTS!

SO LET ME GUESS. YOU WERE ALL INVITED TO A PARTY THAT WENT TERRIBLY WRONG?

AND THAT WOMAN OUT THERE *ISN'T* REALLY BYRA TUSSLE, IS SHE?

"NEEDING THE MONEY TOURISTS WOULD BRING FOR THE TOWN, WE PITCHED IN."

"SHE **TOLD** US SHE HAD THE CAVE TESTED FOR SAFETY, BUT I GUESS WE WERE PRETTY **STUPID** TO BELIEVE THAT!"

"JUST GUESS **WHO** WAS THE ONLY ONE WHO MADE IT OUT?"

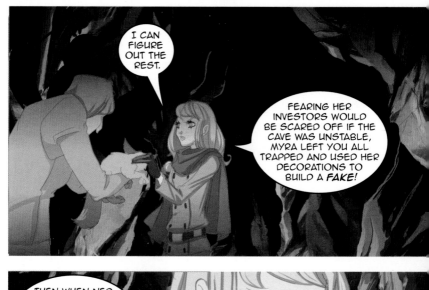

I CAN FIGURE OUT THE REST.

FEARING HER INVESTORS WOULD BE SCARED OFF IF THE CAVE WAS UNSTABLE, MYRA LEFT YOU ALL TRAPPED AND USED HER DECORATIONS TO BUILD A *FAKE*!

THEN WHEN NED AND I SHOWED UP, SHE PRETENDED TO BE HER SISTER, FIGURING IT WAS THE *FASTEST* WAY TO GET RID OF US!

THAT'S WHY SHE DIDN'T WANT US GOING INTO THE BRUSH!

BUT SHE MUST BE *CRAZY* IF SHE PLANNED TO LEAVE US HERE *FOREVER*!

NOT *FOREVER*, JUST LONG ENOUGH TO RUN OFF WITH HER INVESTORS' *MONEY*! IF SHE'S *THIS* DESPERATE, SHE PROBABLY HAS SOME FINANCIAL PROBLEMS OF HER OWN.

WHICH IS PROBABLY WHY SHE NEEDED YOU ALL TO ACT AS HER CLEAN-UP CREW!

I HAVE TO WARN NED ABOUT MYRA-BYRA!

BUT THE CAVE WALLS ARE BLOCKING MY SIGNAL.

HMM? THAT'S NO CRYSTAL REFLECTION. IT'S *MOON-LIGHT*.

BUT WHERE'S IT *COMING* FROM?

A SMALL *HOLE*.

NOT BIG ENOUGH FOR A *PERSON*.

THOUGH I BET IT LOOKED KIND OF CREEPY FROM THE OUTSIDE, LIKE *TALES FROM THE CRYPT*.

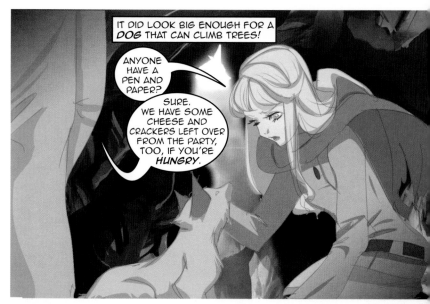

IT DID LOOK BIG ENOUGH FOR A *DOG* THAT CAN CLIMB TREES!

ANYONE HAVE A PEN AND PAPER?

SURE. WE HAVE SOME CHEESE AND CRACKERS LEFT OVER FROM THE PARTY, TOO, IF YOU'RE *HUNGRY*.

NOT RIGHT NOW, THANK-YOU.

I KNEW IT WAS A LONG-SHOT, BUT TOGO HAD ALREADY PROVEN TO BE UNUSUALLY *SMART*.

TOGO, YOU REMEMBER NED, DON'T YOU? THE CUTE GUY FROM THE CAR?

YIP

MEANWHILE, AFTER FRANTICALLY DIGGING IT **FREE** AGAIN, MYRA WAS SHOWING HER RECENTLY ARRIVED INVESTORS HER FAKE CAVE.

BEAUTIFUL! BUT ARE YOU SURE IT'S **SAFE**?

ABSOLUTELY! I HAVE THE REPORT BACK IN THE HOUSE!

UNFORTUNATELY, SMART AS HE WAS, TOGO DID **NOT** FIND NED. INSTEAD HE HEADED STRAIGHT FOR MYRA.

GRRRR!

IT WAS ALMOST AS THOUGH THE LITTLE GUY WANTED TO SOLVE THE CASE HIMSELF!

WHO'S THIS CUTE FELLOW?

THAT? IT'S A... UH... A **DOG**!

GRRRR!

WOULD YOU MIND STANDING, 'MAM?

WE HAVE A FEW *QUESTIONS* WE NEED TO *ASK* ABOUT A *CAVE* ON YOUR PROPERTY.

GOOD OLD NED HAD BROUGHT THE CAVALRY, EVEN *FASTER* THAN I FIGURED

BUT AGAIN, MYRA HAD *OTHER* IDEAS.

THE WHOLE TOWN'S TRAPPED IN A CAVE! OVER THERE! YOU'D BETTER HURRY!

SHE HEADED STRAIGHT FOR THE CEMETERY. I GUESS SHE WAS THINKING SHE MIGHT BE ABLE TO ESCAPE IF SHE REACHED THE *WOODS* ON THE OTHER SIDE.

WHICH PROVIDED A VERY *INTERESTING* OPPORTUNITY FOR ME.

AAHHHHHHHHHHHHHH!!

BYRA, NO! YOU'RE *DEAD!* LET GO! LET GO!

SEE? I *TOLD* YOU IT LOOKED PRETTY CREEPY.

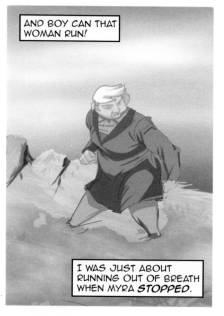

AND BOY CAN THAT WOMAN RUN!

I WAS JUST ABOUT RUNNING OUT OF BREATH WHEN MYRA *STOPPED.*

SEEMS SHE'D COME TO SOMETHING OF A DEAD END.

AND WHEN YOU'RE CHASING SOMEONE, THAT'S A *GOOD* THING, RIGHT?

NOT ALWAYS. ESPECIALLY IF THE PERSON YOUR CHASING CAN DO THINGS LIKE STOP A *CAR* WITH HER BARE HANDS.

REALLY THINK YOU CAN *TAKE* ME, GIRLY?

I FELT THE WAY A *DOG* MUST FEEL WHEN IT CHASES A CAR AND FINALLY *CATCHES* ONE.

WHAT ON EARTH WAS I GOING TO DO WITH IT NOW THAT I HAD IT?

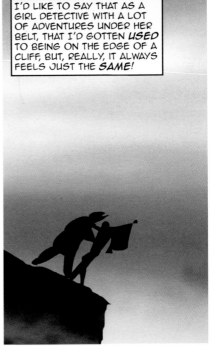

I'D LIKE TO SAY THAT AS A GIRL DETECTIVE WITH A LOT OF ADVENTURES UNDER HER BELT, THAT I'D GOTTEN *USED* TO BEING ON THE EDGE OF A CLIFF, BUT, REALLY, IT ALWAYS FEELS JUST THE *SAME*!

TERRIFYING!

I'LL TEACH *YOU* TO BRING THAT DOG BACK HOME!

BUT IT TURNED OUT, I HADN'T COME *ALONE*!

ACK!

YIP!

TOGO HAD COME TO THE RESCUE!

AH.

AND A FEW HOURS LATER...

YOU BOTH DID A TERRIFIC JOB HERE! YOU MUST BE A REAL ASSET TO YOUR COMMUNITY!

WOULD YOU MIND CALLING CHIEF McGINESS BACK AT RIVER HEIGHTS AND TELLING HIM THAT? SOMETIMES HE THINKS I'M KIND OF A *PAIN*.

WELL, TOGO, I GUESS THIS IS GOOD-BYE! I'M SURE SOMEONE HERE WILL GIVE YOU A GREAT HOME!

OH, NONE OF *US* CAN REALLY *AFFORD* A PET, ESPECIALLY NOW THAT THE CAVE'S BEEN PROVEN TOO *DANGEROUS* FOR TOURISTS. PERHAPS *YOU'D* TAKE HIM.

ME?

YIP!

A FEW DAYS LATER, ANOTHER *STORM* WAS BREWING.

NANCY, I'M *HOME!*

SOLVE ANY MAJOR CRIMINAL CASES WHILE I WAS GONE, LIKE HOW TO GET THE *LIGHTS* BACK ON?

THAT DAD, WHAT A KIDDER! BUT IT WAS FUNNY HE SHOULD MENTION TH

HI DAD!

JUST *ONE* CASE, REALLY, AND, WELL, BECAUSE OF IT, I'VE GOT A LITTLE *SURPRISE!*

REALLY? WHAT SORT OF SURPRISE?

AT LEAST HE DIDN'T RUN *SCREAMING* LIKE HANNAH DID. THOUGH IN A COUPLE OF WEEK EVEN *SHE* WARMED TO HIM, AND TOGO WAS PRACTICALLY ONE OF THE FAMILY!

YIP!

AGHH!

THE EN

This Fall, take the mystery with you
on your Nintendo DS™ system!

NANCY DREW™

The Deadly Secret of Olde World Park

- Play as Nancy Drew, the world's most recognizable teen sleuth
- Solve puzzles and discover clues left by a slew of suspicious characters
- Use the Touch Screen to play detective mini-games and access tasks, maps and inventory
- Unravel 15 intriguing chapters filled with challenging missions and interrogations

MOST FOLKS BELIEVE IN *SOME* KIND OF MAGIC. IT'S FUN TO BE MYSTIFIED BY STUFF THAT SEEMS IMPOSSIBLE.

BUT, I'M NANCY DREW, GIRL DETECTIVE. SO, I'M NOT ONE TO BE *MYSTIFIED* FOR LONG – NOT IF I CAN HELP IT.

I'VE INVESTIGATED LOTS OF "IMPOSSIBLE" THINGS. AND BEHIND MOST MAGIC THERE'S A PERFECTLY EXPLAINABLE...

...TRICK.

CHAPTER ONE:
ILLUSION CONFUSIO

I'VE BEEN A FA... UH, FOLLOWING HIS CAREER EVER SINCE.

AND WELL, HE'S PLAYING HERE! IT WOULD BE NICE TO GO. YOU GUYS INTERESTED?!

WELL, I WAS GOING TO WASH MY HAIR...

YOU *HAVE* TO COME! YOU JUST *HAVE* TO! DAN'S THE BEST. YOU *CAN'T* MISS HIM!

I WOULD, BUT TONIGHT I HAVE A DATE WITH NED!

LOOK I'M NOT KEEPING SCORE, NANCY. BUT, DO I HAVE TO REMIND YOU THAT I RECENTLY FACED A VICIOUS, GROWLING *DOG* FOR YOU?

YES, BUT *NED* RECENTLY RISKED HIS LIFE FOR NANCY, TOO, CLIMBING ON THE ROOF OF A SPEEDING TRAIN.

÷GLUMPF!÷

PLEASE, NANCY?! I'D NEVER ASK THIS ABOUT ANYONE EXCEPT *DAN*.

DON'T MISS NANCY DREW GRAPHIC NOVEL # 14 – "SLEIGHT OF DAN"

Go Undercover in Paris
as Nancy Drew® in
Danger by Design

You, as Nancy Drew, are in Paris to work undercover for a prestigious fashion designer. Minette is all the rage in the fashion world, but strange threats and unwelcome guests are causing her to unravel. It's up to you to stitch the clues together and unmask the mystery in this PC adventure game.

dare to play™

FOR MYSTERY FANS 10 to Adult

Nancy Drew PC Adventure Game #14
Order online at www.HerInteractive.com
Also in stores!
Compatible with WINDOWS® 98/2000/Me/XP/Vista

Created by

THE HARDY BOYS®

NEW GRAPHIC NOVEL EVERY 3 MONTHS!

"The Ocean of Osyria"
N1-59707-001-7

"Identity Theft" ISBN1-59707-003-3

"Mad House" ISBN1-59707-010-6

"Malled" ISBN1-59707-014-9

"Sea You, Sea Me!" ISBN1-59707-022-X

"Hyde & Shriek" ISBN 1-59707-028-9

"The Opposite Numbers..."
N 1-59707-034-8

"Board to Death" ISBN 1-59707-053-X

"To Die, Or Not To Die?"
N 1-59707-062-9

N! #10 "A Hardy Day's Night"
N 1-59707-070-X

Pocket sized, 96-112pp., full color, $7.95
available in hardcover! $12.95 each.

dy Boys
ed Set #1-4

pages of color comics!
95
1-59707-040-8

dy Boys
ed Set #5-8

pages of color comics!
95
1-59707-075-0

OTALLY SPIES!

"The O.P." ISBN 1-59707-043-2

"I Hate the 80's" ISBN 1-59707-045-9

"Evil Jerry" ISBN 1-59707-047-8

"Spies in Space" ISBN 1-59707-055-6

: 5x7 1/2, 112pp., full color paperback: $7.95
available in hardcover! $12.95 each.

PAPERCUTZ.COM

WATCH OUT FOR PAPERCUT𝕑™

If this is your very first Papercutz graphic novel, then allow me, Jim Salicrup, your humble and lovable Editor-in-Chief, to welcome you to the Papercutz Backpages where we check out what's happening in the ever-expanding Papercutz Universe! If you're a long-time Papercutz fan, then welcome back, friend!

Things really have been popping at Papercutz! In the last few editions of the Backpages we've announced new titles such as TALES FROM THE CRYPT, CLASSICS ILLUSTRATED, and CLASSICS ILLUSTRATED DELUXE. Well, guess what? The tradition continues, and we're announcing yet another addition to our line-up of blockbuster titles. So, what is our latest and greatest title? We'll give you just one hint -- the stars of the next Papercutz graphic novel series just happen to be the biggest, most exciting line of constructible action figures ever created! That's right -- BIONICLE is coming! Check out the power-packed preview pages ahead!

Before I run out of room, let me say that we're always interested in what you think! Are there characters, TV shows, movies, books, videogames, you-name-it, that you'd like to see Papercutz turn into graphic novels? Don't be shy, let's us know! You can contact me at salicrup@papercutz.com or Jim Salicrup, PAPERCUTZ, 40 Exchange Place, Ste. 1308, New York, NY 10005 and let us know how we're doing. After all, we want you to be as excited about Papercutz as we are!

Thanks,

Jim

EDITOR-IN-CHIEF

Caricature drawn by Steve Brodner at the MoCCA Art Fest.

TWO DOZEN TEEN DETECTIVE GRAPHIC NOVELS NOW IN PRINT!

You know, while it's exciting to be adding so many new titles, we don't want anyone to think we've forgotten any of our previous Papercutz publications! For example, can you believe there are now two dozen all-new, full-color graphic novels starring America's favorite teen sleuths?! Let's check out what's happening in the 12th volume of NANCY DREW…

Writers Stefan Petrucha and Sarah Kinney and artists Sho Murase and Carlos Jose Guzman present Nancy's latest case, "Dress Reversal." After

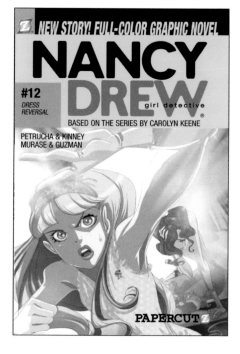

showing up at River Height's social event of the year, in the identical dress as the party's hostess, Deirdre Shannon, things get worse for Nancy when she's suddenly kidnapped! That leaves Bess, George, and Ned to solve the mystery of the missing Girl Detective.

That's all in NANCY DREW #12 "Dress Reversal," on sale sale at bookstores everywhere and online booksellers.

Behold. . .

At the start of the new millennium, a new line of toys from LEGO made their dramatic debut. Originally released in six color-coded canisters, each containing a constructible, fully-poseable, articulated character, BIONICLE was an instant hit!

The BIONICLE figures were incredibly intriguing. With their exotic names hinting at a complex history, fans were curious to discover more about these captivating characters. Even now, over six years later, there are still many unanswered questions surrounding every facet of the ever-expanding BIONICLE universe.

A comicbook, written by leading BIONICLE expert and author of most of the BIONICLE novels Greg Farshtey, was created by DC Comics and given away to members of the BIONICLE fan club. The action-packed comics revealed much about these mysterious biomechanical (part biological, part mechanical) beings and the world they inhabited. A world filled with many races, most prominent being the Matoran. A world once protected millennia ago by a Great Spirit known as Mata Nui, who has fallen asleep. A world that has begun to decay as its inhabitants must defend themselves from the evil forces of Makuta.

The first story arc of the comics called "The BIONICLE Chronicles," begins when six heroic beings known as Toa arrive on a tropical-like island which is also named Mata Nui. The Toa may just be the saviors the people of Mata Nui need, if they can avoid fighting with themselves, not to mention the Bohrok and the Rahkshise early comics are incredibly hard-to-find, and many new BIONICLE fans have never seen these all-important early chapters in this epic science fantasy. But soon, those comics will be collected as the first two volumes in the Papercutz series of BIONICLE graphic novels.

These early comics are incredibly hard-to-find, and many new BIONICLE fans have never seen these all-important early chapters in this epic science fantasy. But soon, those comics will be collected as the first two volumes in the Papercutz series of BIONICLE graphic novels.

In the following pages, enjoy a special preview of BIONICLE graphic novel #1…

I HAVE SLEPT FOR SO *LONG. MY DREAMS* HAVE BEEN *DARK* ONES.

BUT NOW I AM *AWAKENED.*

NOW THE SCATTERED ELEMENTS OF MY BEING ARE REJOINED.

NOW I AM *WHOLE.*

DON'T MISS BIONICLE GRAPHIC NOVEL # 1 "RISE OF THE TOA NUVA"

CLASSICS
Illustrated

Featuring Stories by the World's Greatest Authors

Returns in two new series from Papercutz!

The original, best-selling series of comics adaptations of the world's greatest literature, CLASSICS ILLUSTRATED, returns in two new formats--the original, featuring abridged adaptations of classic novels, and CLASSICS ILLUSTRATED DELUXE, featuring longer, more expansive adaptations-from graphic novel publisher Papercutz. "We're very proud to say that Papercutz has received such an enthusiastic reception from librarians and school teachers for its NANCY DREW and HARDY BOYS graphic novels as well as THE LIFE OF POPE JOHN PAUL II...*IN COMICS!*, that it only seemed logical for us to bring back the original CLASSICS ILLUSTRATED comicbook series beloved by parents, educators, and librarians," explained Papercutz Publisher, Terry Nantier. "We can't thank the enlightened librarians and teachers who have supported Papercutz enough. And we're thrilled that they're so excited about CLASSICS ILLUSTRATED."

Upcoming titles include The Invisible Man, Tales from the Brothers Grimm, and Robinson Crusoe.

FULL-COLOR GRAPHIC NOVEL ADAPTATION

CLASSICS *Illustrated* *Deluxe*

THE WIND IN THE WILLOWS

By Kenneth Grahame

Adapted by
Michel Plessix

PAPERCUTZ

A Short History of CLASSICS ILLUSTRATED...

   William B. Jones Jr. is the author of Classics Illustrated: A Cultural History, which offers a comprehensive overview of the original comic-book series and the writers, artists, editors, and publishers behind-the-scenes. With Mr. Jones Jr.'s kind permission, here's a very short overview of the history of CLASSICS ILLUSTRATED adapted from his 2005 essay on Albert Kanter.

CLASSICS ILLUSTRATED was the creation of Albert Lewis Kanter, a visionary publisher, who from 1941 to 1971, introduced young readers worldwide to the realms of literature, history, folklore, mythology, and science in over 200 titles in such comicbook series as CLASSICS ILLUSTRATED and CLASSICS ILLUSTRATED JUNIOR. Kanter, inspired by the success of the first comicbooks published in the early 30s and late 40s, believed he could use the same medium to introduce young readers to the world of great literature. CLASSIC COMICS (later changed to CLASSICS ILLUSTRATED in 1947) was launched in 1941, and soon the comicbook adaptations of Shakespeare, Stevenson, Twain, Verne, and other authors, were being used in schools and endorsed by educators.

CLASSICS ILLUSTRATED was translated and distributed in countries such as Canada, Great Britain, the Netherlands, Greece, Brazil, Mexico, and Australia. The genial publisher was hailed abroad as "Papa Kassiker." By the beginning of the 1960s, CLASSICS ILLUSTRATED was the largest childrens publication in the world. The original CLASSICS ILLUSTRATED series adapted into comics 169 titles; among these were Frankenstein, 20,000 Leagues Under the Sea, Treasure Island, Julius Caesar, and Faust.

Albert L. Kanter died, March 17, 1973, leaving behind a rich legacy for the millions of readers whose imaginations were awakened by CLASSICS ILLUSTRATED.

CLASSICS ILLUSTRATED was re-launched in 1990 in graphic novel/book form by the Berkley Publishing Group and First Publishing, Inc. featuring all-new adaptations by such top graphic novelists as Rick Geary, Bill Sienkiewicz, Kyle Baker, Gahan Wilson, and others. "First had the right idea, they just came out about 15 years too soon. Now bookstores are ready for graphic novels such as these," Jim explains. Many of these excellent adaptations have been acquired by Papercutz and will make up the new series of CLASSICS ILLUSTRATED titles.

The first volume of the new CLASSICS ILLUSTRATED series presents graphic novelist Rick Geary's adaptation of "Great Expectations" by Charles Dickens, the bittersweet tale of one boy's adolescence, and of the choices he makes to shape his destiny. Into an engrossing mystery, Dickens weaves a heartfelt inquiry into morals and virtues-as the orphan Pip, the convict Magwitch, the beautiful Estella, the bitter Miss Havisham, the goodhearted Biddy, the kind Joe and other memorable characters entwine in a battle of human nature. Rick Geary's delightful illustrations capture the newfound awe and frustrations of young Pip as he comes of age, and begins to understand the opportunities that life presents.

BY LATE AFTERNOON, WE REACHED A RESTING PLACE BELOW GRAVESEND, WHERE THE RIVER IS BROAD AND SOLITARY. THERE WE SPENT THE NIGHT, NERVOUS AND EXPECTANT OF WHAT WAS TO COME.

IN THE MORNING, WE ROWED TO THE RIVER'S MIDDLE, INTENDING TO HAIL THE STEAMER BOUND FOR HAMBURG, OR THE ONE FOR ROTTERDAM...

PIP, LOOK!

IT WAS A POLICE GALLEY, CLOSING IN QUICKLY TO CUT US OFF. ON BOARD WAS A PRISONER WITH HIS HEAD COVERED.

HO THERE! YOU HAVE A RETURNED TRANSPORT—HIS NAME IS MAGWITCH, OTHERWISE PROVIS! I CALL ON HIM TO SURRENDER!

Here is one preview page of CLASSICS ILLUSTRATED #1 "Great Expectations" by Charles Dickens, as adapted by Rick Geary. (CLASSICS ILLUSTRATED will be printed in a larger 6 1/2" x 9" format, so the art will be bigger than what you see here.)